I0821617

Computer Programming

FROM ADA LOVELACE TO MARK ZUCKERBERG

Kelly Doudna

An Imprint of Abdo Publishing
abdopublishing.com

ABDOPUBLISHING.COM

Published by Abdo Publishing, a division of ABDO, PO Box 398166, Minneapolis, Minnesota 55439. Checkerboard Library™ is a trademark and logo of Abdo Publishing.

Printed in the United States of America, North Mankato, Minnesota
052018
092018

Design and production: Mighty Media, Inc.
Editor: Liz Salzmann
Cover Photographs: iStockphoto (right), Shutterstock (middle), Wikimedia Commons (left)
Interior Photographs: Alamy, pp. 15, 19; Arnold Reinhold/Wikimedia Commons, pp. 24, 28 (bottom); iStockphoto, p. 4–5; JD Lasica/Flickr, pp. 21, 29 (bottom); Marcin Wichary/Flickr, pp. 17, 23, 29 (top); Science Museum/Science & Society Picture Library, p. 7; Shutterstock, p. 27; US Navy/Wikimedia Commons, pp. 9, 11, 13, 28 (top)

Library of Congress Control Number: 2017961639

Publisher's Cataloging-in-Publication Data
Name: Doudna, Kelly, author.
Title: Computer Programming: From Ada Lovelace to Mark Zuckerberg / by Kelly Doudna.
Other titles: From Ada Lovelace to Mark Zuckerberg
Description: Minneapolis, Minnesota : Abdo Publishing, 2019. | Series: STEM stories | Includes online resources and index.
Identifiers: ISBN 9781532115455 (lib.bdg.) | ISBN 9781532156175 (ebook)
Subjects: LCSH: Computer programmers--Juvenile literature. | Computer Science--Juvenile literature. | Software engineering--Juvenile literature. | Inventors--Biography--Juvenile literature.
Classification: DDC 005.1092--dc23w

Contents

Computing Life

Do you take your smartphone everywhere? Do you keep in touch with your friends using **social media** apps? Do you have a hard time imagining life without the internet? This lifestyle is possible because of computers and the programs that run on them!

The invention of the computer arose from the need to quickly process information. At its most basic, information was processed by adding and subtracting numbers. In the early 1640s, Blaise Pascal invented a mechanical calculator and manufactured it for sale. The machine was known as the Pascaline.

Many schools and clubs offer classes to teach kids about computer programming.

Over time, computing machines improved. This was thanks to mathematicians and inventors such as Charles Babbage, Ada Lovelace, and Herman Hollerith. However, these machines were mostly mechanical.

In the mid-1900s, electronic computers were developed. This led to the need for programming languages and programmers. Computer scientists including Grace Hopper, Steve Jobs, Tim Berners-Lee, and Mark Zuckerberg made today's computers and programs possible.

CHAPTER 1

Programming Preview

Charles Babbage was an English mathematician and inventor. In 1834, he designed the Analytical Engine. It was a calculating machine. It could be programmed using cards with holes punched in them. The positions of the holes provided information and instructions to the machine.

Babbage never finished building the Analytical Engine. Nevertheless, it is recognized as the first concept for a general-purpose computer. For this reason, Babbage is sometimes referred to as the father of computing.

English mathematician Ada Lovelace was Babbage's student. She had a deep understanding of the Analytical Engine. In 1843, Lovelace translated an article about the Analytical Engine from French

FUN FACT

Punched cards were based on a system developed by French weaver Joseph-Marie Jacquard. In the early 1800s, Jacquard created a method of using punched cards to control the weaving pattern of looms. Looms operated this way were known as Jacquard looms.

into English. Lovelace added her own lengthy notes to the work. Her notes included an **algorithm** for programming the Engine to compute **Bernoulli numbers**. This algorithm is widely considered to be the first computer program.

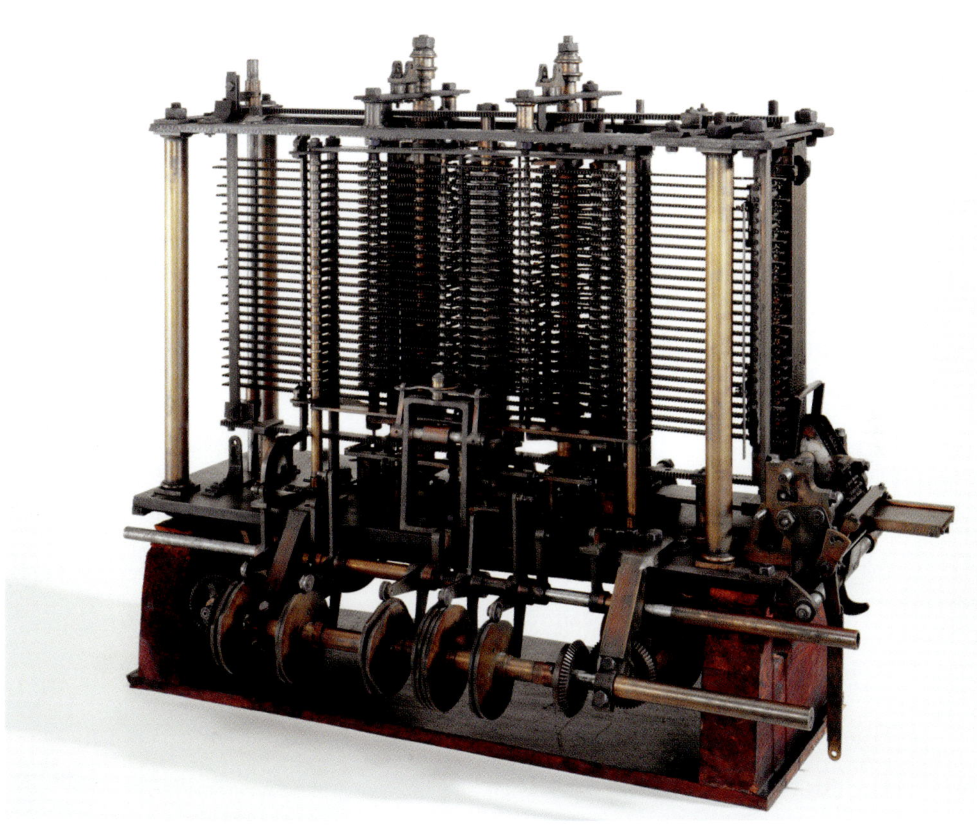

A portion of Babbage's Analytical Engine can be viewed at the Science Museum in London.

Though Lovelace's work was important, it was largely forgotten for the next hundred years. In the meantime, American inventor Herman Hollerith built a device to tally the 1890 US **census**. Cards punched with census data were fed into the **tabulating** machine. The positions of the holes on each card represented different pieces of census information.

This information included where people lived, how old they were, and more. In addition to being merely counted, the data could be sorted in different ways. Hollerith's tabulating and sorting machine was an important step forward in computing.

English mathematician George Boole developed an important foundation for programming in 1847. He created what is now known as Boolean **logic**. Boolean logic uses operators such as "AND," "OR," or "NOT" to determine whether statements are true or false. This causes certain actions. For example, if a statement is false, a different action is performed than if the statement were true.

FUN FACT

Herman Hollerith founded the Tabulating Machine Company in 1896. It was purchased and merged with several others in 1911. This formed the Computing-Tabulating-Recording company. In 1924, C-T-R was renamed International Business Machines, or IBM!

Ada Lovelace

BORN: December 10, 1815, London, England

DIED: November 27, 1852, London, England

FACT: Lovelace's full name at birth was Augusta Ada Byron.

FACT: Lovelace was the daughter of the poet Lord Byron.

FACT: Lovelace was educated in math and science, which was unusual for women of her

ACHIEVEMENTS

- When Lovelace was 12, she designed a steam-powered flying machine.
- Because of her **algorithm** for calculating **Bernoulli numbers**, Lovelace is considered by many to be the first computer programmer.
- Lovelace saw possibilities beyond the Analytical Engine's basic function of calculating numerical results. She proposed that it could process any information which could be expressed mathematically. This included music and **graphics**.

STEM Star

CHAPTER 2

Hefty Hardware

Advances in computer hardware came fast in the mid-1900s. **World War II** started in 1939. It spurred development of computers for use in the war. Each side wanted better **technology** to help defeat its enemies.

In 1941, German engineer Konrad Zuse completed the Z3 computer. It was the first programmable computer. The programs were stored on punched film that the computer could read. The programming made it the first fully **automatic** computer.

The next major advancement was the Colossus computer. It was designed by British engineer Tommy Flowers to decode **Nazi** messages. It was completed in 1944. The speedy performance of the Colossus gave the **Allies** an advantage. This is credited with shortening the war.

Around the same time, scientists and engineers at the University of Pennsylvania were developing a computer called ENIAC. This was the first electronic computer used for general functions, such as solving math problems. The project began in

1943 but wasn't completed until after the war, in 1946. ENIAC was used by the US government to perform calculations for building nuclear bombs.

ENIAC was made of 40 **panels**. Each panel was 8 by 3 feet (2.5 by 1 m) and arranged in a *U* shape. ENIAC filled an entire room. It was the fastest, most **complex** machine at the time.

ENIAC had thousands of parts. It could complete 5,000 additions per second!

CHAPTER 3

Terrific Transitions

Early computers, such as the ENIAC, used programs written specifically for them. The programs couldn't be transferred to different machines. This changed with the development of high-level programming languages. These languages could be used to program different types of computers.

One of the first high-level languages was FORTRAN, released in 1957. FORTRAN was used to perform computations such as weather forecasting. It is still used today in many scientific fields.

FORTRAN and other early languages used codes that included strings of numbers and symbols. Computer scientist Grace Hopper believed that a computer language could use English words rather than codes. She thought this would make it easier for businesspeople to understand and use computers.

Hopper's idea led to the development of the programming language COBOL in 1959. COBOL was used mainly to process information for businesses, such as financial data. It was widely used up to the 1990s.

Computer program capabilities took a big step forward in 1967. This is when Simula 67 was released. It was developed in Norway. Simula 67 introduced concepts that led to object-oriented programming.

Grace Hopper learned computer programming in the US Navy. By the end of her military career, she had achieved the rank of rear admiral.

With an object-oriented language, a computer program is not just a list of instructions for the computer. Instead, the program is made up of individual pieces, or objects. Objects can interact with one another and be reused in different programs. With Simula 67, **complex** programs were easy to create and maintain. If a change was needed, only the affected object needed to be updated.

CHAPTER 4

Fast Forward

In the 1960s and 1970s, computer hardware improved greatly. Computers went from being big enough to fill a room to small enough to sit on a desk. Computers also got much faster.

In 1962, computer scientists at England's University of Manchester completed the Atlas computer. Atlas introduced the idea of an operating system. This is a separate set of instructions that ran the basic functions of the computer.

Computers also started becoming less expensive to own. In the past, only government, military, and science institutions could afford to have computers. Now, more individuals were able to buy their own computers. Computer engineers began to focus on improving the experience of computer users.

Key to this was how the computer operator programmed the computer. ENIAC and Colossus used batch processing. All commands were programmed first and then run in order. This changed in the 1960s. Computers started using command-line interface.

The Atlas computer was considered to be the fastest computer in the early 1960s.

Command-line interface allowed users to interact with programs as they ran. Users could enter commands that the computer would execute immediately. Command-line interface gave users more control over how computers operated.

CHAPTER 5

Great Graphics

Now that the computer had more capabilities, engineers gave more attention to the user interface. In 1968, American engineer Douglas Engelbart presented his **online** system called NLS. It was the first computer that allowed people to share screens and edit files at the same time.

In the early 1970s, American computer scientist Alan Kay released the object-oriented programming language Smalltalk. It ran on the Xerox Alto computer. Smalltalk created a user-friendly interface. Smalltalk featured menu bars, desktop icons, and individual windows that scrolled. These types of elements make up a computer's **graphical** user interface (GUI).

American businessman Steve Jobs and computer scientist Steve Wozniak founded Apple Computer in 1976. The Apple team further developed the GUI. The team added features such as the trash can, double-clicking, and drag-and-drop. Apple's GUI was introduced to the public with the release of the Apple Macintosh computer in 1984.

The first Apple Macintosh computer cost $2,500. In the first three months after its release, 50,000 Apple Macintoshes were sold.

Apple's main competitor was computer company Microsoft. Microsoft created operating systems for other manufacturers' computers. In 1985, Microsoft released its own GUI operating system, Windows. By the mid-1990s, the Apple and Microsoft systems were the most successful.

CHAPTER 6

Incredible Internet

Computers had become faster and easier to use. Engineers and computer scientists started developing new tasks that could be accomplished using computers. Easily sharing information over a **network** became a big goal. And the internet would become the biggest network!

Developments that led to the internet began in the 1960s. That's when American computer scientist Ted Nelson began working on Project Xanadu. Xanadu was a system in which information could be stored and then retrieved by different computers.

Nelson coined the term "hypertext" in the 1960s. This was the structure of links used to connect to and find information in the system. Nelson and a team worked into the 1970s to develop Xanadu, but they were never completely successful. However, Nelson's concept of hypertext represents the basis of the internet.

The next step toward the internet was ARPANET. This was a computer network created by the US government's Advanced

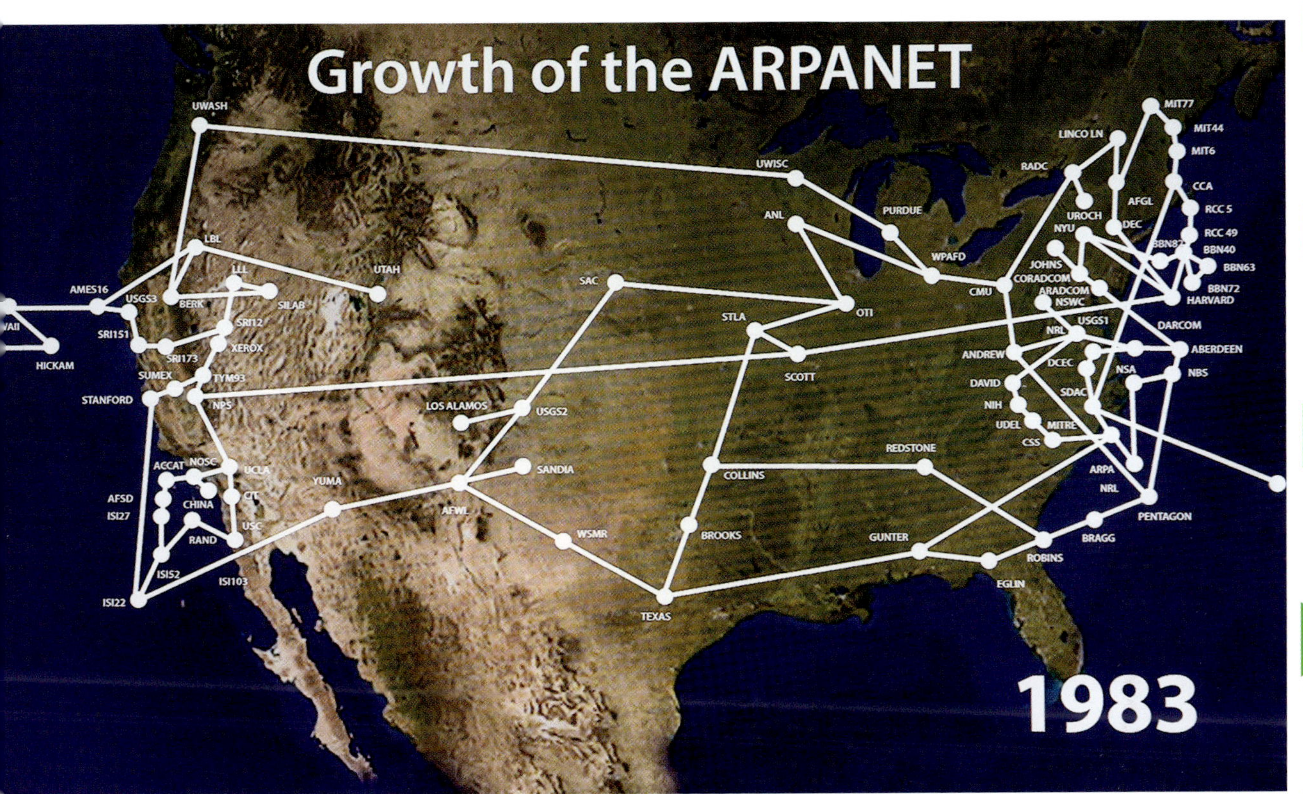

In 1969, four computers were connected to ARPANET. By the 1980s, computers across the United States were connected. ARPANET was retired in 1990.

Research Projects Agency in the late 1960s. ARPANET was the first **network** to successfully link multiple computers. The network continued to grow as more and more computers were added. It started being called the internet in 1983.

In 1989, British computer scientist Tim Berners-Lee developed hypertext transfer protocol (HTTP). HTTP standardized how computers talked to one another over **networks**. It provided a set of rules for file and information transfer.

Much of the information exchanged over the internet took the form of web pages. Berners-Lee also invented hypertext mark-up language (HTML). HTML is the programming language that tells **web browsers** what web pages should look like.

Together, pages of related content became known as websites. Individuals and companies could have websites. Berners-Lee called the system that contains these websites the World Wide Web, or "the web." People connect to the web to view and share websites.

Many websites served communities of people with shared interests. A user had his or her own profile page and interacted with other members of the community. Common interests ranged from music to photography to business. Some websites were simply used for socializing.

One such social site is Facebook. American programmer Mark Zuckerberg and three college friends worked on this project in college. They launched Facebook in 2004. By 2009, Facebook had more users than any other social networking website.

Mark Zuckerberg

BORN: May 14, 1984, White Plains, New York

FACT: Facebook also owns two other popular websites, Instagram and WhatsApp.

FACT: Mark Zuckerberg created his first messaging program when he was 12 years old. He called it "ZuckNet."

ACHIEVEMENTS

- Zuckerberg was named *Time* magazine's Person of the Year in 2010.
- Zuckerberg made the Fortune 500 list in May 2013. At 28 years old, he was the youngest CEO on the list.
- In 2015, Zuckerberg and his wife, Priscilla Chan, announced the Chan Zuckerberg **Initiative**. Chan and Zuckerberg will give 99 percent of Facebook's shares to this charity.

STEM Star

CHAPTER 7

Mobile Might

As more users were connecting on the web, computers became smaller and more personal. This change in computer size began in the early 1980s, when **portable** computers first appeared. In 1991, Apple Computer released the Macintosh PowerBook. It was a popular notebook-sized computer.

Mobile telephones had also been shrinking in size while gaining capabilities. The first smartphone was released by IBM in 1994. But at first, mobile **networks** were only fast enough to make calls and send texts. As the networks got faster, smartphones allowed users to send photos, stream videos, and more.

Another type of computing device being developed was the tablet. In 1972, Alan Kay proposed a tablet computer called the Dynabook. It was planned to be an educational tool for children. But **technology** at the time wasn't advanced enough to make building it possible. The first successful tablet was the Apple iPad. It came out in 2010. The iPad was soon joined by tablets from other manufacturers.

Alan Kay doesn't think any invention has come close to his Dynabook prototype. He believes tablets today are just devices for consuming media rather than learning.

Smartphones and tablets changed the way people used computer applications, or "apps." With just a few taps, users could **download** apps from their devices' **online** store. **Social media** apps were especially popular. Users no longer had to sit at a computer to check in with their friends.

Programming:
PAST AND PRESENT

Computer programming started with punch cards. The position of each hole indicates a different piece of data. Today, programmers use programming or mark-up languages, such as HTML. These languages use tags, brackets, and other symbols.

PUNCH CARD

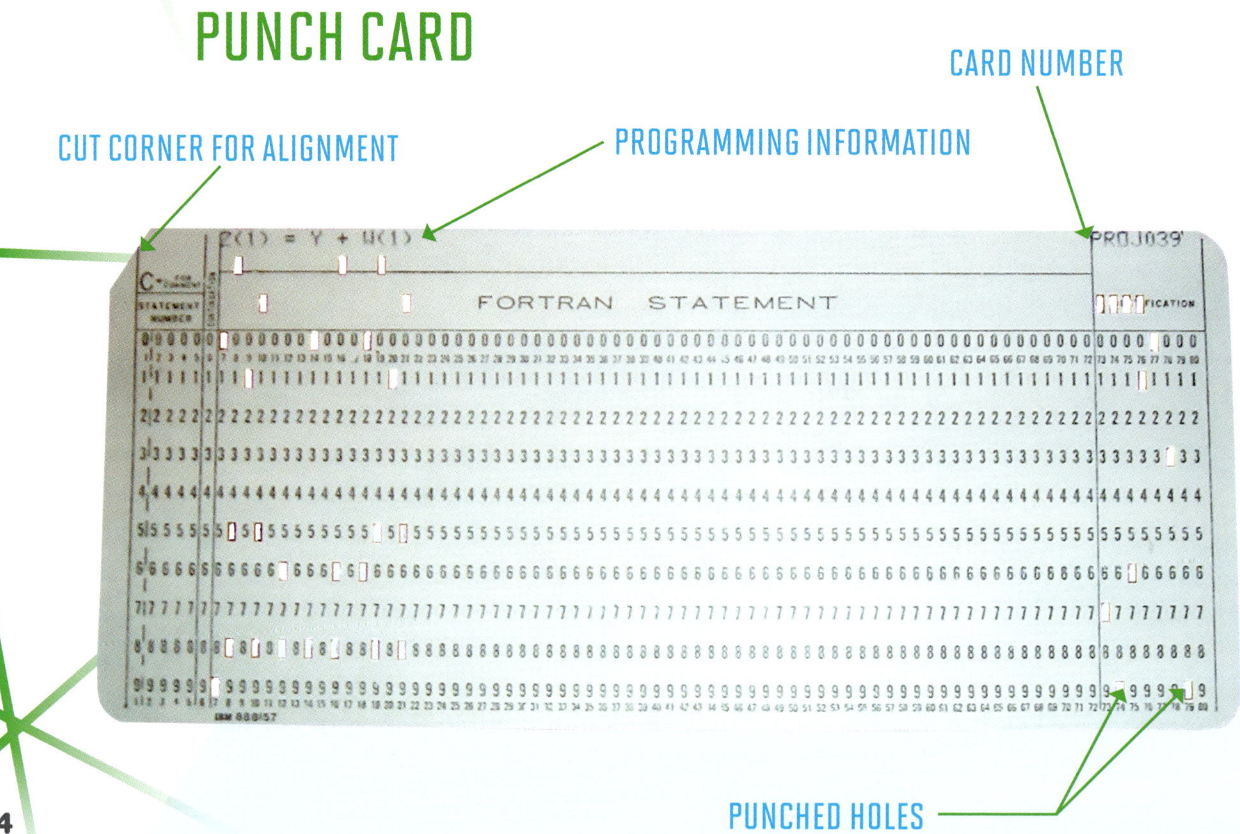

HTML CODE

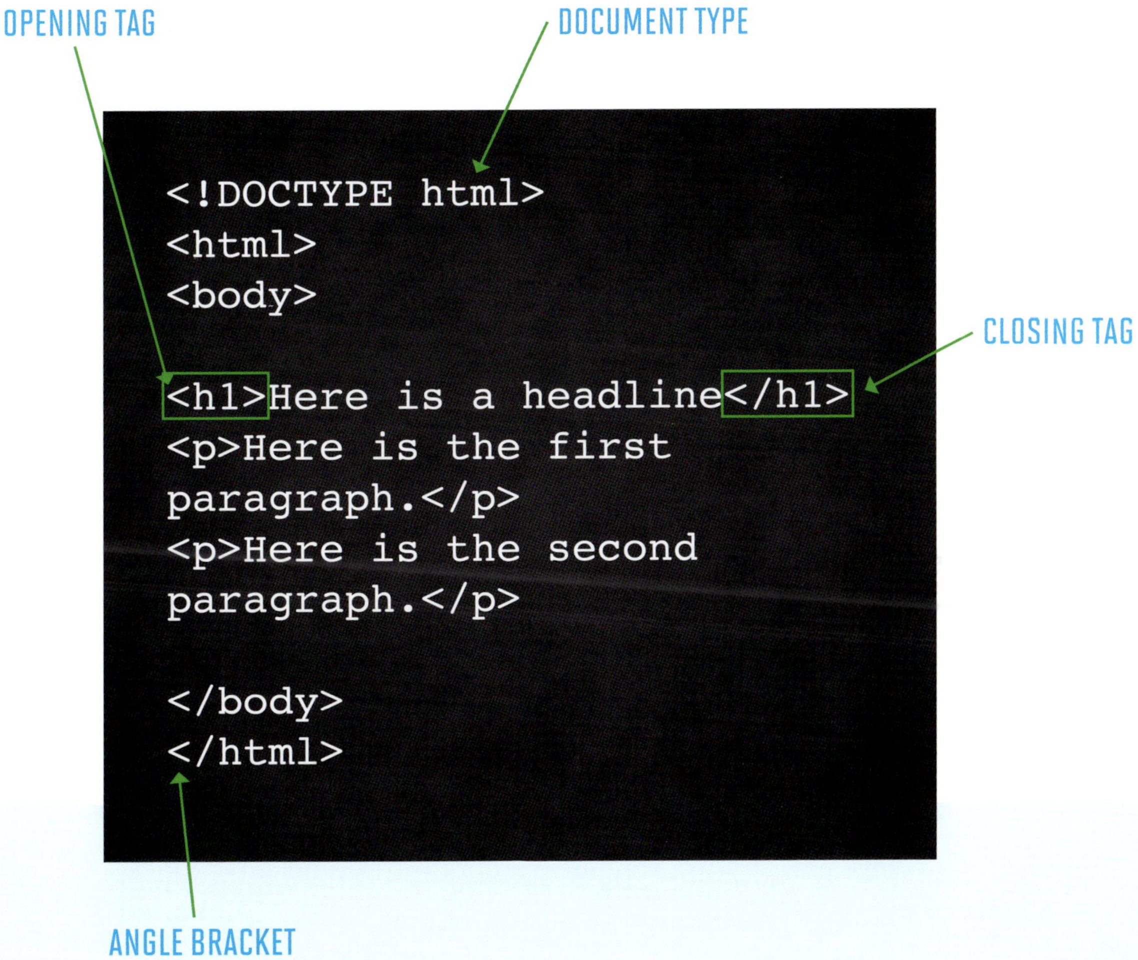

OPENING TAG

DOCUMENT TYPE

CLOSING TAG

```
<!DOCTYPE html>
<html>
<body>

<h1>Here is a headline</h1>
<p>Here is the first
paragraph.</p>
<p>Here is the second
paragraph.</p>

</body>
</html>
```

ANGLE BRACKET

CHAPTER 8

A Future in the Cloud

In addition to mobile devices with exciting new features, another development in computer programming is called cloud computing. This is when users work with applications and data stored on central servers known as "the cloud" rather than on their own devices. The cloud allows programmers to work from anywhere.

It's likely that more software development will happen in the cloud. Programmers will create applications that are native to the cloud and used only there. Soon, software will no longer be kept on users' own computers. Instead, users will do all of their computing on the cloud.

Computer education will change too. People will no longer need computer science degrees to learn programming. Children will learn how to write computer programs from an early age.

Another computing trend is the Internet of Things (IoT). The IoT consists of computerized devices that connect directly to the internet. These devices include household **appliances**, cars, and

Amazon Echo Dot is an example of an operating system for the Internet of Things. The device responds to voice commands to provide information, shop online, play music, and more. It does so through a cloud-based service called Alexa.

security systems. They connect to the internet so people can use them remotely or to **automatically** receive updated software. Some experts believe that there could be 30 billion devices on the IoT by 2020.

The growing number and types of computerized devices means that the need for software to run them will also increase. And all of these programs will require more and more skilled programmers. They will create the computing marvels of the future!

Timeline

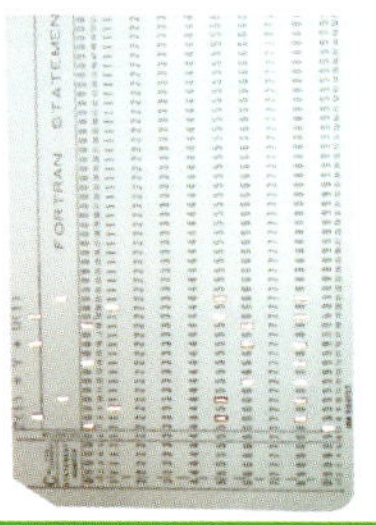

1834 Charles Babbage designs the Analytical Engine.

1843 Ada Lovelace translates an article about the Analytical Engine. She adds notes about using it to compute Bernoulli numbers.

1941 Konrad Zuse completes the Z3, the first programmable computer.

1957 The programming language FORTRAN is released.

1967 Simula 67, is released, leading to object-oriented programming.

1968 Douglas Engelbart presents the NLS online system.

1976 Steve Jobs and Steve Wozniak found Apple Computer.

1983 The computer network ARPANET starts being called the internet.

1989 Tim Berners-Lee creates HTTP, HTML, and the World Wide Web.

2004 Mark Zuckerberg and three college friends launch Facebook.

Glossary

algorithm—step-by-step instructions for solving a mathematical problem or to completing a computer process.

allies—people, groups, or nations united for some special purpose. During World War II Great Britain, France, the United States, and the Soviet Union were called the Allies.

appliance—a household or office device operated by gas or electric current. Common kitchen appliances include stoves, refrigerators, and dishwashers.

automatic—moving or acting by itself.

Bernoulli numbers—a series of numbers that are calculated by a mathematical formula developed by Jakob Bernoulli.

census—a count of the population of a certain area.

complex—having many parts, details, ideas, or functions.

download—to transfer data from a computer network to a single computer or device.

graphics—pictures or images on the screen of a computer, smartphone, or other device.

initiative—a plan or program that is intended to solve a problem.

logic—the science dealing with rules of correct reasoning and with proof by reasoning.

Nazi—the political party that controlled Germany under Adolf Hitler from 1933 to 1945.

network—a system of computers connected by communications lines.

online—connected to the internet.

panel—part of a flat surface such as a wall or screen.

portable—able to be carried easily.

social media—forms of electronic communication that allow people to create online communities to share information, ideas, and messages. Facebook, Instagram, and Snapchat are examples of social media.

tabulate—to count and record in an orderly way.

technology (tehk-NAH-luh-jee)—machinery and equipment developed for practical purposes using scientific principles and engineering.

web browser—a computer program providing access to sites on the World Wide Web.

World War II—from 1939 to 1945, fought in Europe, Asia, and Africa. Great Britain, France, the United States, the Soviet Union, and their allies were on one side. Germany, Italy, Japan, and their allies were on the other side.

Online Resources

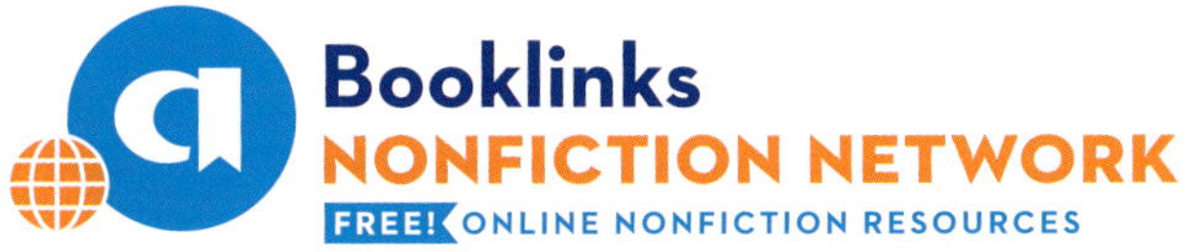

To learn more about computer programming, visit **abdobooklinks.com**. These links are routinely monitored and updated to provide the most current information available.

Index